For my sister, Marian ~ M. D.

For Charlie and Jordan ~ J. V.

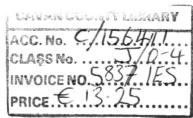
ABOUT THE STORY

I got the idea for Sleepy Pendoodle *from a story that I first came across in a collection of Irish folk tales by Professor Henry Glassie, whose scholarly and highly enjoyable studies of folklore have given me much inspiration as a writer.*

M. D.

Published 2002 by Walker Books Ltd, 87 Vauxhall Walk, London SE11 5HJ

10 9 8 7 6 5 4 3 2 1

Text © 2001 Malachy Doyle
Illustrations © 2001 Julie Vivas

This book has been typeset in ITC Tempus Sans

Printed in Italy

British Library Cataloguing in Publication Data:
a catalogue record for this book is available from the British Library.

ISBN 0-7445-7508-7

Sleepy Pendoodle

Malachy Doyle   illustrated by Julie Vivas

WALKER BOOKS
AND SUBSIDIARIES
LONDON • BOSTON • SYDNEY

I was out down the alley,
   and I found a wee pup.
A funny little, bonny little,
   lost little pup.

I brought him home
and I fed him with a bottle.
But I had him for a week
and he never opened his eyes,
not once.

I went to see
    my Uncle Hughie,
and I asked him
    what to do.

"You scrubby-scrub
your hands,"
said Hughie,
"and you put him
on your knee.

You stroke him on
the back and say,

'Open your eyes,
    Sleepy Pendoodle!
Open your eyes,
    you pup!'

Will you
    remember that?"

"I'll try," I said.

So I ran all the way home, shouting,
"Pendoodle,
        Pendoodle,
Pendoodle!"
because that's the bit
    I thought I might forget.

"What's the hurry?"
said Annie O'Donnell.
"Pendiddle,
        Pendiddle!"
    said I.

"Where's the fire?" said
Doctor Fitzgerald.
"Pendaddle,
Pendaddle!"
said I.

"What are
you doing?"
said Molly
and Mart.
"Penduddle,
Penduddle!"
said I.

So I got home, said hello to my pup, and I tried to remember what my Uncle Hughie had told me.

I scrubby-scrubbed my knees, and I held him in my hands.

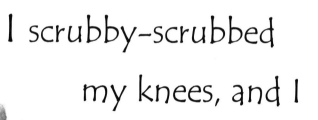

I stroked him once,
I stroked him twice,
and I said,

"Open your eyes,
Sloppy Popwaddle!
Open your eyes, you pup!"

But he didn't open his eyes.

So I scrubby-scrubbed
my pup,

I stroked my bony knees,

I put him on my back and said,

"Open your eyes,
   Peepy Splendiddle!
Open your eyes,
     you pup!"

But he still didn't open his eyes.

Oh, what did Uncle Hughie say?
Oh, what did Hughie say?

So I scrubby-scrubbed
my hands, till there wasn't
a speck of dirt on them.

I plumped myself down
in my granny's chair,
and I put him on my knee.

I told him what a fine
young pup he was …

and I stroked him

ever-so-cosy,

all the way down his back,

from his flippy-flop ears

to the end of

his fluffy little tail.

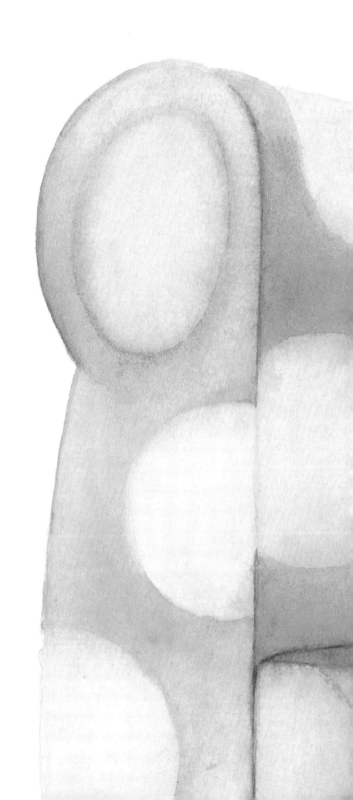

And when I'd done all that I said,

"Open your eyes,
        Sleepy Pendoodle!
Open your eyes, you pup!"

His whiskers quivered,
his body shivered …

and he opened his eyes wide!

He looked into
my face and yelped.

And when I popped
him down,

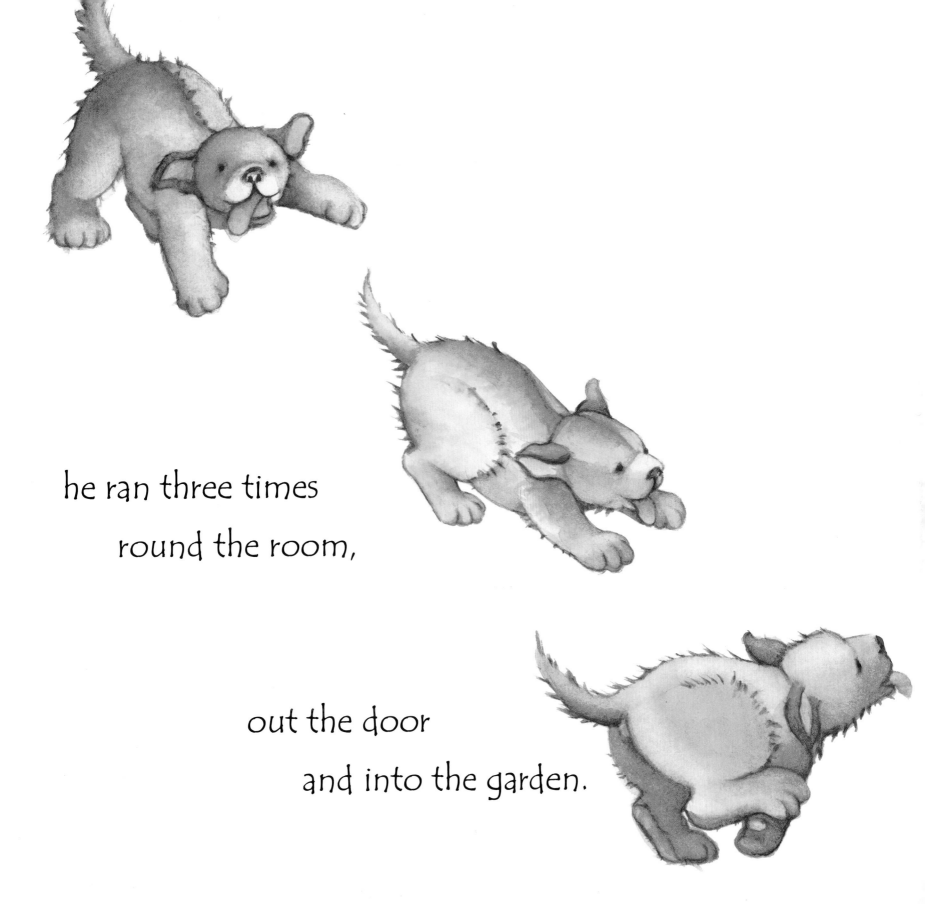

he ran three times
round the room,

out the door
and into the garden.

I chased out after him,
      and he was yapping and yelping
and licking my face,
      and wagging his tail like
      a mad thing!

My Pendoodle.

And now he's a
big
red
dog.